The Murder At Cliff Hanger Lodge

David Evans

Table of Contents

One day there was a lodge, the lodge was called Cliff Hanger Lodge and is situated between two mountains in Colorado. On the other side of the mountain, there was a sheer cliff. The lodge was built in the early eighties and is beginning to fall apart due to not being cared for. The owner of the lodge was a wealthy man whose name was Alvin.

He worked as an investor on Wall Street and is from a wealthy family. He was born and raised in Ireland, and when he was twenty-nine years old, he moved to Colorado in 1982 and had the lodge built in the mountain. It took two years for the lodge to be completed, when it was done, he popped open a glass of champagne and shared it with the builders.

Alvin had five workers and got along well with all of them. The lodge has two floors and even has a built-in elevator, the elevator was custom and was made out of a hard wood. He uses the elevator to lift heavy things up to the second floor. In the lodge there are a total of five rooms, and there are three bathrooms.

The counter tops in all the bathrooms are marble, Alvin wouldn't have it any other way. He likes everything that he does to be done first class. However, Alvin had been thinking about enlarging the lodge, but wasn't sure how he wanted to enlarge the lodge. He had a well-known architect whose name was Wesley.

Chapter One: The Beginning

Wesley has worked as an architect his whole life; his father was also an architect. Wesley is not cheap to hire, in fact it cost Alvin $600,000 just to have Wesley come out and give him building ideas.

The day after he talked to Wesley, Wesley had received a phone call from a Prince in Saudi Arabia and had to take a flight out there for a day and never returned Alvin phone calls. Alvin was getting increasingly irritated with his friend Wesley and after six days of no communication and not getting a call back, he decided that it was time to fire Wesley.

It was late afternoon and Alvin called Wesley anyway, he left a voice mail on Wesley's machine. Now this was the seventh day and still no reply or call back. Alvin was beginning to wonder if his friend had just disappeared. Wesley had a nice private jet and a collection of land rovers, which he cherished so much.

Alvin moved on and found another architect whose name was Brian. Alvin was on his laptop one late night and had come across Brian's name as he was checking his emails. Alvin likes to have the best in everything and says that's how he likes it. Alvin has never been interested in looking for a woman to date, but instead would rather work the rest of his life.

His mom and dad had called him and asked him if was going to have any kids and he told them no and I don't care for kids. The conversation quickly got argumentative and his mom and dad hung up on him. Alvin like some people does not get along well with his parents.

Although is still kind of afraid of his father, when he was a little boy, he would run around the kitchen making silly faces and screaming while his dad was trying to cook. His dad would take off, his belt and hit him with it if he wouldn't, stop screaming. To this day he doesn't like to wear belts or even look at them.

His dad would make him work hard and wouldn't reward him for doing a good job. This is the first time in two years that he was on the phone with his father. While Alvin still has a good relationship with his mom, and they haven't saw each other in a year.

Alvin's mom and dad do not visit him, but instead makes him visit them. The lodge makes Alvin a lot of money, and he likes to save his money. One year he treated himself and got himself a brand-new truck and a private jet. The private jet cost him almost two million dollars, and he wanted the interior redone which cost half a million dollars.

Alvin is worth eight million dollars and wants to someday to be a billionaire. In the back of the lodge there is a secret room, to get to it you have to know where to push on the bookshelf to make it turn and then it leads you into the room. The bookshelf looks like a conventional bookshelf.

There are four shelves on the bookshelf and each one is packed with books on survival and hunting and trapping. There's a large metal safe in the back of the secret room, and in it are a collection of long rifles and old cowboy style wild west forty-five caliber pistols. This collection of firearms wasn't cheap and cost him a whopping thirty grand.

At the back of the lodge is a shooting range. Alvin takes his favorite guns out each day for a good hour and a half. This gun range was here even before he decided to make the lodge.

He hadn't constructed the gun range, but the previous landowner had made it. After he's done shooting his guns, he cleans them off with a gun cleaning spray. The spray smells bad and sometimes makes him sneeze.

One day after he was done shooting, a thought came into his mind, he thought to himself why don't I hire a butler. He walked into his bedroom and opened up his laptop and looked online for a butler.

He looked through a list of ten men who were butlers and took time to read about each of them and their personality traits and after fifteen minutes he made a decision. He saw a guy named Leo and read all about him and figured that he would be a good fit.

He pulled out his smart phone and began to dial the number, the phone rang twice, and Leo picked up.

"Hello, whom is this?"

"My name is Alvin, and I was calling about your butler ad."

"What would you like to know?"

I would like to know if you would mind leaving your home in Washington and coming to work with me here in Colorado.

The call went quiet for a moment and Leo and asked how good the pay was? Alvin said I will pay you ever how much you decide. I would like forty-five thousand dollars, each day to work for you.

"Is that okay with you?"

"It's alright, I will pay you that then."

"How soon can you get a flight, out here to my lodge?"

"I can get on a plane tomorrow; would that be okay with you?"

"That's fine with me."

"Is there anything special that I have to bring with me?"

"No," just bring yourself,

"Do you have kids?"

"No, and I'm not married, I live with my friend at their house.

You seem like you are getting irritated with me, I'm not getting irritated with you. It's just I want to know if I will have my own room, of course you will have your own room. Okay thank you for telling me. I can't wait to meet you Alvin, me either Leo.

"Do you like to drink?"

"Yes," I do.

I only like to drink fine wine. I'm a beer kind of guy and I sometimes get sick when I drink too much. Actually one time I drank a case of beer, and you know I didn't even remember what had happened that night.

I'm going to have to get going, and I will see you when I see you.

"Do you have enough money to get a plane ticket?"

"No," actually I have a friend, whose a pilot, and he owns a small plane.

I will call him right after we hang up, okay Leo a good rest of the day. Alvin hung the phone up and walked back outside to the gun range and gathered up the rest of the guns and put them away back in the gun safe.

He locked up the gun safe and carefully closed the safes door and walked out of the room and closed the secret door. Alvin was feeling dry, he opened a small cabinet, and pulled out a small glass full of brandy and poured some into a shot glass. He took a sip of it and made a sour face.

He then shook his head and said that was good and poured another shot. He put the brandy bottle away in the cabinet. On the property he has two big ski lifts and two big fireplaces at either end of the lodge. He had a custom deck made alongside the left side of the lodge. The deck's made out of pine wood and some oak boards here and there.

There are a bunch of trees right outside of the lodge. He had specially sent for pine trees, because there weren't enough pine trees that he could find in the immediate area. Instead there were a lot of oak trees, and Alvin doesn't like pin oak trees, he doesn't like that acorns fall from the trees. He loves the smell of fresh pine tree sap.

If he gets time, he likes to make custom pine comb Christmas trees. It takes him a great deal of time to complete just one pine comb Christmas tree. He decorates the pinecone Christmas trees with white lights. He likes to keep his hands clean, so he wears gloves while working on the pinecone Christmas trees.

He sits at a huge wooden table; the table is so big that it just about takes up the whole room. There are custom extenders built into the table. He takes an old newspaper and places it down first before he starts to work on the pinecone Christmas tree. Over the years he has made twenty-two pinecone Christmas trees.

Alvin has given his pinecone Christmas trees to his friends and family. He even gave one to his mother and to this day she still has it. She loves how it lights up and placed in on a table by her bay window. However, she hasn't bothered it with in so many years that it has a thick layer of dust on it.

Alvin used to like to carve things out of wood, but since the accident that he had last year, he has had second thoughts on starting up his wood carving business. He was cutting up wood and his coat sleeve got caught on the piece of wood that was going down the table to the table saw.

Thinking fast he took out his sharp pocketknife and cut his coat right off before he was pulled into the blade. He quickly ran behind the machine and switched it off before it cut up his coat. His father had bought the coat for him and he is still upset that he ruined it. Ever since he doesn't even get near the table saw and doesn't even dare to turn it on.

It's been three years since that incident, and he had placed the table saw back in storage. His lodge is open to the public and anyone who's older than eighteen years is welcome. Each day a few skiers come in to visit the lodge and ski on his many mountain slopes. He has fifteen different slopes to choose from. Some of the slopes are steeper than others and this makes them more dangerous.

He has a name for each slope, and at the front desk the quests must sign in or cannot stay at the lodge. He's very strict about his rules and doesn't like when families bring their babies with them. He's always worried for their safety. There's a special room where he lets the quests put their babies while they are skiing.

He watches over the babies while he is sitting behind the front desk. Some of the babies are so bad and just keep on crying out and this doesn't seem to bother him too much. There's a lot to do around the lodge and it's too much work for just one man, so Alvin was forced to hire a repair man to fix up his ski lifts when they would break down.

The repair man's name is Elmer, he's a young guy in his early thirties, and works well with Alvin. Alvin also has a bookkeeper and supervisor; his bookkeepers name is Scarlet. She's a kind woman who loves her job, she works there nine to five each day. Alvin's always pleased with how well she keeps his taxes and other finances in such good order. Callie is the supervisor, and watches what everyone's doing at any given time.

Alvin doesn't like to have cameras monitoring people, but to keep his business open the state had him install two cameras. He had to pay for the cameras himself, the two cameras cost him just under three thousand dollars. He had bought the state-of-the-art cameras; these cameras came equipped with night vision and had auto zoom. They were even waterproof and shatter proof.

It just took him two hours to hang up both cameras. Elmer helped him to hang them up, Callie's thirty-eight years and loves working at the lodge. She has been working at the lodge for five years ever since it was constructed. She prefers not to wear makeup, because she says that she's allergic to make up.

While Scarlet's much younger and wears too much makeup and her skin then reacts to it and pimples form on her forehead. She wears nice work clothes and doesn't like to wear dresses. She was wears nice dress shirts and pants to Match. She has long brown hair and sometimes likes to dye her hair all black.

One day she walked in, and Alvin doesn't recognize her at first because her hair was jet black. She is slim and likes to wear black dress shoes, and always packs her own lunch. Alvin's odd though, because he doesn't like to eat in the same room that his staff does. Instead he eats his lunch at his desk.

Alvin was eating lunch at his desk and a little boy came walking over to him and said hey.

"Do you know where my parents went?"

"No." I don't know little boy, but I can look for them.

"Where did you last see them?"

"He pointed out the window and said I saw them walking that way."

Chapter Two: Cause For Alarm

Alvin stopped eating his lunch and helped the little boy. I will call Callie my supervisor and see what she's doing and have her start looking for them. Please don't wonder away from me, I'm trying to help you.

"Can I hold your hand until my parents get back?"

"Yes," you can if that makes you feel better.

The little boy's little hands were cold

"What's your name little boy?"

"My name is Harmon"

It's nice to have met you Harmon, my name is Alvin, and I'm the owner of this place. Alvin got on his walkie talkie and paged Callie. Callie please pick up, she picked up and asked what was the matter, I'm sitting in the waiting room with a little boy named Harmon, and he can't seem to find his parents.

"Could you please come in here and supervise him?"

"I sure will"

Just hold on a moment and I will be in. Alright, don't worry we will find your parents. But I'm scared, there's no reason to be scared I'm right here and will protect you.

"Are there any wolfs or bears around here?"

"Yes," there is but you shouldn't worry about them.

"What's your dads first name"

"His first name is Shawn and his last name?"

"Wesson."

"Alright how about your moms first name?"

"Her first name is Kelly and has the same last name.

"Callie walked in and seemed to be out of breath.

"What's wrong Callie?"

"It's so cold out there."

That you could freeze if you don't keep moving. This is the second time this has happened in a week; I'm getting concerned about how this lodge is being run.

"Did you call me in here just to argue with me?"

"No," I didn't, I just need help and I am concerned.

I will find his parents and If him and I are not back in two hours then I want you to call the authorities

"Is that clear?"

"Yes," it is,

Go back to sleep and let me do my job. Yes, I do have an attitude today just to let you know. I wasn't going to say anything about that. I will be back soon. Good luck, thanks and she stormed out of the lodge. Alvin got up off of the couch and watched outside, all of a sudden, the wind began to pick up and there was a blizzard.

The visibility was terrible, and you could hear the wind howling. Alvin sat down by the fireplace and warmed up his cold hands and feet. The tip of his nose was cold to the touch and so were his hands. But he kept is eyes focused out the big window. All he could see where large snowflakes.

Right outside the window was a wooden picnic table. It was already covered in an inch of snow and the snow doesn't seem like it was going to subside. Alvin was beginning to get worried.

At the lodge there are four snow machines and two snow cats. There are four big garages on the property, each shed is heated and locked up when the conditions get too bad like on a day like this. Alvin thought to himself I'm going to take some matters into my own hands and go out into the garage and get in a snow cat and go searching for them. Then Scarlet walked into the room and had a tired look on her face.

Alvin looked at her and she said well I'm not feeling good today, I just got out of the bathroom after throwing up twice. I'm sorry to hear that Scarlet. I wanted to know if there was any chance that I could leave work early today.

"Would that be, okay?"

"That would be okay."

"Did you take a look outside lately?"

"No," I haven't

I don't think that you want to leave in here in a middle of a blizzard.

"It's bad out there."

"What are you doing?"

"I'm just thinking about what I'm going to do next."

I hope you aren't going to go out there, yes, I was actually thinking about it. What!

"Do you have a death wish?"

"No," but I'm concerned.

Yes, but at a time like this it's best to stay in here where's it nice and warm. I agree but I have to get outside eventually.

"Where's Callie?"

"She's out there looking for a kids parents."

"Wait why?"

"A little boy came to me and told me he lost his parents."

"How did he lose his parents?"

"I don't know why I didn't ask him everything about what had happened."

Alright I got to go back to the bathroom, I will talk to you later, sounds good. Alvin looked over at the clock on the wall and it was slowing ticking away. Now it was almost an hour since Callie had gone looking for the kids parents.

He put his head back and began to feel himself falling asleep. He didn't want to fall asleep. He happened to open his eyes and saw that it was fifteen more minutes until two hours had gone by. He pulled out his smart phone and was on the dialing screen, and his hands began to tremble and shake.

He pressed the nine key, then went on to press one and another one. He looked at the right-hand corner of the screen and saw that the reception wasn't so good. Just then Elmer came walking into the room

> "What's going on?"

> "We have an emergency."

> "What do you mean an emergency?"

> "Callie has gone missing"

> "How long?"

> "For two hours now."

I would wait another hour then call 911. No, Callie told me that after two hours and that if she wasn't back then I should call the authorities. I have the local Police phone number.

> "Would you like it?"

> "Yes."

He cleared out the dial area in his phone. I'm ready, it's 414-243-587. Thank you so much, once Alvin dialed the number it rang twice and a guy with a low voice picked up.

> "Who's this?"

> "My name's Alvin, and I was I calling to report a missing person."

My name is Rob, and I'm the only officer who's in the area right now.

> "When can you come out and take a look around?"

> "I need assistance right away."

Alright, why don't you calm down, and I will be out when I can. I don't know if that means a day or a week. Look Pal our Policemen have been really busy around here lately.

“Why’s that?”

“I would like to tell you that, but I can't, it's against the law.”

I love my job and don't want to lose it. Now tell me the name of the person or persons that went missing. It's a middle-aged woman whose name is Callie, and is

She’s in really good shape. Because if you live in Colorado you better be strong and be used to the cold. She knows how to deal with the cold weather and besides that she has been working up in the mountains for five years. You don't have to tell me all that.

“What has you in such a mood?”

“To start with I have to watch over two departments and I should only be working one department with help”

My helper’s on vacation for a week. I’m a good Police Officer, and I wouldn’t do anything wrong.

“How long has she been missing for?”

“She has been missing for almost three hours now.”

“Can you tell me her exact words that she said to you before she left?”

“Yes,” I can

She said If I’m not back in two hours then call the authorities and that's exactly what I did. I’m happy that you are being so honest to me. You know there’s a bad blizzard going on outside and it's making me more concerned about her.

“Do you think you can, come out to my lodge in an hour?”

“I will see what I can do, and I will have to give you a call back in an hour.”

We don't have that kind of time, we may never find her if we don't start looking now. I don't want to go looking around out in a blizzard for a missing person, but I would rather wait until the blizzard is over. This person’s in need of help right now. I’m sorry I cannot come out right now. I mean what if she was in an avalanche and is freezing to death. That isn’t fair to her, look life isn’t fair and never will be.

“Could you please change your mind and come up here?”

“I will come over right now”

Thank you so much, I really appreciate this. You're welcome, I will be there. Talk to you soon, bye now.

"What did the Officer say?"

"He was being stubborn."

I had to straighten him out, you know I appreciate all you do for me and the lodge. You always keep the bathrooms clean and I appreciate that. I hope that they can find Callie and the little boy's parents.

Forty-five minutes later, Rob pulls into the parking lot, in a brand-new pickup truck with an extended cab. Alvin walked over by the front of the lodge and looked out the large main window.

Rob quickly got out of his truck and walked over to the front door of the lodge. Alvin opened the door and let Rob in. Hi, it's good to have finally met you, likewise.

"Has anyone gone missing from here in the past year?"

"No," and this is the first time.

Rob had a thick black mustache and had large muscular arms. He had his Tuger 9 millimeter strapped to his belt. He had a flashlight latched on his belt on his left side. He wore wolverine boots, and brown work pants and shirt.

"Where did you see her last?"

"She had walked out back here and never returned."

"That sounds suspicious and was there anyone else with her?"

"Yes," a little boy.

"How old was he?"

"He was ten years old."

"Do you have a surveillance system?"

"Yes," I do

"Where's your command room?"

"It's down the hallway off to the left, I will let you in."

You can take a seat if you would like, no that's okay I would rather stand anyway, and besides that I'm trying to lose weight. You have a lot of computer screens in here.

"How many are there?"

"There are a total of eight computer screens in here and they are all high-definition screens."

"Is there any way that you can, rewind the tapes?"

"Yes," I can, give me a moment to log into the system.

"How long is that going to take?"

"Just five minutes hold on."

"After you are done showing me the tapes?"

"Can I take a look around in the rooms and upstairs?"

"You sure can Officer."

You know, I think I might have forgotten the password to log in.

"How did you do that?"

"I don't know it just slipped my mind"

If you don't mind, I'm going to have to ask my helper what it is. Hold on I will be right back, I need your help.

"Why are you shouting for me?"

"It's something important that I need help with."

I forgot the password to get into the computer system

"Do you know the password?"

"Yes," then follow me into the control room.

I will, let me introduce you to Officer, hi Rob my name is Elmer and it's nice to have met you, likewise. You are a quick Typer, can you tell me what you just typed. The password is Bluejay95,

"Now are you going to remember the password this time or should I write it down for you?"

"I would appreciate it if you wrote it down."

Thanks again. Now you are logged into the system, thanks so much. You're welcome, anytime. Now let's go through the tape and review it well.

"Do you usually sit in here and watch the tapes?"

"No," I don't Elmer usually watches it every day.

Rob put his right hand on Alvin's right shoulder.

"Is my hand bothering you there?"

"No," it's okay

I don't see anything out of the ordinary happening on any of the tapes. I'm not sure what's going on here. I have seen enough video and tapes for now. I want to take a walk around the lodge now.

"Are you going to take me around the place or is Elmer going to?"

"I will Officer."

This is a really nice lodge, and is well kept, and I like the deer head mounts on the walls. I especially like the Bob cat mount, I bet that mount cost a pretty penny, yes in fact it cost me $1,650.

I like whole body mounts, and this one is unique. I appreciate you commenting on the mounts.

"Did you shoot some of those deer?"

"Yes," I went hunting with a friend on a few occasions.

I'm a hunter too, and I have a large collection of firearms.

"Are they large caliber guns?"

"No," I have a few twenty-two caliber rifles and a few handguns.

"What kind of handgun calibers do you have?"

"I have one classic wheel gun"

"Do you have any 9mm pistols?"

"Yes," I have one or two of them.

"How often do you go out to the range and practice?"

"I try to get out to the range every other day."

"That's a good thing"

"How about you?"

"I work every day and barely have time for myself."

"Do you have any kids?"

"No," not yet but I plan to in the future

"Are you married?"

"No," I just have a girlfriend for now.

I have a big family and my dad used to be a Police Officer too, and he's now retired from the force.

"How many years was he a Police Officer?"

"He was on the force for ten years, that's a long time."

My father now spends his time resting at home, and with age he now has bad knees and can't walk well. I'm sorry to hear that. It's alright, he will be okay and it's just how it is when you get old.

"How many skiers come here to ski every day?"

"Five skiers every day, and business has been great lately."

As of lately there have been bad blizzards occurring around here.

"You are on the top of the mountain"

"What do you expect?"

That's true, but don't talk smart to me. I don't appreciate that.

I'm sorry that I commented. I can see that you have nothing to hide and if you don't mind, I will now go outside and look around for Callie and the kid. Good luck officer, I will be back in a few minutes, and don't worry I know the trails around here and I won't get lost.

Rob carefully closed the door behind him, and Alvin was feeling on edge. He began to chew on his fingers nails on his left hand. Then Elmer walked into the room, and he had a frown on his face.

"What's the matter?"

"I'm feeling tired and need to rest, it's getting late. I don't think I will be able to do any over time tonight."

That's alright, I didn't expect you to. Alvin happened to look down at his wristwatch, and it showed that it was going on six thirty at night. You are here past your shift.

"Did you realize that?"

"No," I didn't realize that it was six thirty at night.

You may go, and you can write down that you worked an extra half an hour, and I will pay you for it. It's so great to work for you, bye now. Alvin looked out the big bay window, at the left side of the lodge.

The sky was all black and there were a few stars in the sky. Alvin felt his right hand and saw that his ring on his four finger was slipping off of his finger. He took the ring off and placed it in his back pocket. He thought to himself I'm glad that I didn't lose the ring.

Alvin looked at the thermostat next to the fireplace and it showed that it was seventy-five degrees. All of a sudden Alvin heard a gunshot that was near the lodge. This shook him up and made him sweat, he stayed sitting behind the front desk. Alvin was thinking to himself, I hope nothing bad happened.

Chapter Three: More To Come

Suddenly the door went flying open and Rob walked in, he was out of breath, and couldn't even get a word out. His face was all red and he was sweaty.

"What happened?"

"You don't want to know, why not?"

What happened out there is so serious and I don't want to go through it again.

"Did you see Callie or the kid?"

"No," I didn't, I didn't even see tracks near any of the trails. I did see large bear tracks and mountain lion tracks.

"Where were the footprints?"

"They were near the sky lifts and the trails."

What made you shoot, I almost got mauled by a mountain lion. I was quietly walking along the one trail and a mountain lion leaped into the air and luckily, I was able to make a good shot to stop him. The mountain lion died right after I shot him in the chest, and he landed on me. I didn't realize just how heavy a mountain lion was.

"How old was the mountain lion"

"It was a young one?"

"It was probably just four years old."

"What did you do with the mountain lions body"

I dragged it and threw it in the back of my truck.

"Aren't you going to get into trouble overshooting the mountain lion?"

"No," I had to shoot him in self-defense.

"Do you think that the mountain lion may have attacked them?"

"Yes," there's a good chance that he did.

"Was it hard to see out there?"

"No," my flashlight is LED and has never let me down.

It's a mag light and I accidentally ran it over once and nothing happened to it. It was so cold out there, I thought that I was going to freeze, but my coat still kept me warm though.

"Are your hands cold?"

"Yes," they are even though I was wearing gloves.

"What kind of gloves do you wear?"

"They are made from leather and some other material."

"Where did you get them from?"

"I bought them from a hardware store."

Meanwhile in Miami, the Gallo Luxury lodge was teeming with out-of-town visitors who were going to stay for a week. Lennon and his wife Stef were comfortably relaxing in there room, occasionally sipping on their wine. When they heard something come crashing down in a room next door to them.

"Do you think we should check it out Dear?"

"No," I don't think so.

Someone may have just dropped something heavy, I'm not so sure about that. If something did happen the police will take care of it. You can't always rely on the police hun. You know how I feel about guns, I don't think they're necessary. I have to disagree with you on that. I don't think we need to get into someone else's business.

Besides that I still have another sip of wine left, you're too laid back hun. I'm not going to be finishing my wine, so you can gladly have the rest of it. We can't go out there in our pajamas we have to look presentable. By the time you're done talking whatever happened will be over. Stef swung open the door and went to the room off to the right to them and knocked on the door.

"Is everything alright in there?"

"There was no answer."

"A brawny man opened the door."

"What are you doing here Ma'am?"

"Checking on you."

I heard a loud crashing sound coming from your room. The man tried to grab her but she turned around and ran down the hall as fast as she could. People in the lobby looked over at her as she feverishly swung open the door.

She slipped on the wet pavement and went down on her side. A car pulled in and an older gentleman got out and seen her and helped her up, thank you for helping me up.

"Are you sure you're okay Ma'am?"

"Yes."

The gentleman walked off and entered the discount store. She quickly ducked behind a pick-up truck when she saw the run through the lobby. She thought to herself I hope that I can escape alive. The man stood by the door looking out for her, her leg began to cramp up. To alleviate the pain she sat down and straitened her leg out. She thought that the man was coming towards her and crawled under the truck and grabbed onto the frame.

To her horror someone got into the truck and started it up, she held on for dear life as the truck went down the road. She could barely hold on and began to scream out and slam on the truck. Eventually the truck came to a complete stop, the man got out and bent down on his knee. He baffled to see a woman under his truck. She franticly looked at the man, with a tear running down her rosy cheek. Ma'am you can come out of there, I'm not going to hurt you.

"How long have you been under my truck?"

"Not very long."

"Should I call someone for you?"

"No."

Come sit in my truck where its warm and continue with what you were saying. He carefully draped an orange blanket over her. I escaped a killer; I think that he killed someone last night. If I wouldn't have run, I would have been his next victim.

"Are you a Police Officer?"

"No," Ma'am.

I'm just a hired hand working on a ranch. I've been working with cattle for two years now, and the owner of the ranch gave me a day off last week, that was nice of him.

"Are you single Ma'am?"

"No."

I've been married for five years now. I still choose to be single man, that's a nice wedding ring on your finger, thank you very much. I don't wear jewelry unless I'm going to a convention. The man brought his arm up and rubbed his unshaven chin.

"Is your husband looking for you?"

"No," not yet.

I love my husband but he's too laid back sometimes. He's probably still in the hotel room watching television and drinking.

"Has he always drank a lot?"

"No."

I will gladly take you back to the lodge. No, thanks. The lodge is a long walk away from here, you better call a cab. She stepped out of his truck and waved to him as he drove away. She went over to a fence and leaned on it, while pondering what she was going to next.

She began to walk towards a strip mall, the parking lot was packed with cars. Several people crossed the road, and a guy on a motorcycle sped past them. As she was crossing Marble Rd, she saw a man wearing a black hoodie holding a baseball bat.

He walked over to a parked car and began beating it up, just keep walking Ma'am. The man who owns his car owes me money. Go ahead run off before I change my mind, she ran towards a crowd of people. One of the people gave her a dirty look as he walked away, she just ignored it. She entered a shoe store, the people behind the desk looked over at her.

"Do you need any help finding anything today?"

"No," thanks I'm just browsing.

We have three new kinds of sneakers, and we have new baseball jerseys. If you buy two shoes you can get thirty percent off, no, thanks Ma'am. I'm in no big rush to buy anything, I'm currently worried for my well-being, a man tried to attack me.

"Ma'am where are you going now?"

"To hide behind this desk back here."

I'm afraid someone's going to attack me, I'm here and I'll protect you. Suddenly four men in hoodies entered the shoe store and shouted out we are protesters and are protesting because our boss has declined to up my wages, now I don't have enough money to feed my family.

Sir, you, and your friends aren't welcome in this store if you're going to protest and destroy our merchandise. One of the men pulled out a knife and held it by one of the workers throats, if anyone of you say another word, I will cut her throat.

Everyone went silent, but two people were whispering in each other's ear. Another one of the protestors pulled out a gun and opened fire and shot up shoes and other merchandise. One of the customers tried to run out and was shot in the back and collapsed onto the floor.

One of the cashiers, was holding her ears and was trembling in fear. Eliz the Police cars are coming this way, take the money from the cash register and let's get out of here.

He let go of the terrified woman and put his knife away. Him and his possie ran frantically down the sidewalk to their getaway vehicle. One of the men had lost their shoe, but they just sped off.

The woman who was attacked took out her phone, and began texting someone while the Police Officers walked in. Everyone came out there of hiding spaces, you are all safe now.

One of the Policemen called in for two medical transports. Stef didn't come out of hiding, she turned on her cell phone to check the time. Eventually the Police finished up there reports, and the medical transports hauled the injured people away. Ma'am if you don't come out, we are going to lock up the store with you still inside.

Okay then enjoy your stay here, we're leaving. They existed the store and went back to their vehicles. Stef stood up and dialed her husband's number and it just ran continuously. She thought to herself what if something happened to him.

She ran over to the door, and there was a lock on it. She left out a heavy sigh and scavenged around the room looking for something to break through the window with.

There was a shopping cart beside the window, but she just passed by it. Instead she walked over to a chair and picked it up and took it over by the window. With all of her strength she picked up the chair and threw through the window. The shops alarm started blaring, she quickly got out of there and went down the street.

Three people on bicycles went past her. One of the cyclists turned around and came back her way. Ma'am you are looking flushed to me, he handed her a bottle of water. There's no need to give it back to me you can keep it.

What brings you to this part of the town?

"It's a long story."

I haven't taken a rest for so long. I think that you better take a seat here for a few minutes and catch your breath.

"What happened to your clothes?"

"I fell into a puddle."

I'm embarrassed enough having to be out here in my pajamas. Someone was chasing me and it didn't have time to change. No, worries I'm not going to judge you. He took out a pen and a piece of paper and wrote down his phone number and gave it to her. If you ever need help or just need to talk you can call this number. I don't like seeing anyone in distress like you were.

"Where's your significant other?"

"I don't know."

He could be dead for all I know. I like to ride bicycle with my friends every day, and we have an extra bike if you would like to join us sometime. That would be great.

"Where are you headed now Sir?"

"To the local diner"

Chapter Four: Uncomfortable

I like to drink their freshly brewed coffee. Speaking of coffee, I'll gladly get you a cup of coffee. That's a nice gesture but no, thanks, I'm sure your girlfriend wouldn't appreciate that. She doesn't need to know who I meet on a daily basis. It sounds to me that you don't share enough with her.

"Do you get into many arguments with each other?"

"No," we don't.

I hate to just leave you here Ma'am, you should come with us. In just a few hours I've seen some very scary things happen. You don't have to worry we won't hurt you. I just want to talk to you some more, you seem like my kind of people. You have a hesitant look on your face. It surely took you awhile to agree with me, now let's go. All of them walked a block over to the diner.

There were many cars in the parking lot, there was an elderly man trying to help his wife to get out of the car. She thought about helping him but decided not to, and walked on by. Most of the seats were filled up with people, in your corner of the room a little girl was sitting beside her teddy bear and smiling.

There was an old man sitting at a table alone, he was sipping on his coffee and looking around the room. Hold on everyone wait to be seated, the waitress had a flustered look on her face. The inside of the diner smelled like a fresh brewed cup of coffee. This is the busiest I've seen this place in a week, anything that you order on the menu here is good.

Do they have chocolate milk here?

Yes, they do.

That waiter back there has a mean look on her face, she's usually like that. Hopefully we don't get her as a waiter today, because she's awfully snippy. A young man waiter came walking over to them, and took them over to a vacant table. Once they all sat down he handed them a menu, today's soup special is tomato soup.

What does everyone want to drink?

Coffee, and she would like some chocolate milk.

I'll be back with your drinks shortly, it's odd how that waiter doesn't look us in the eyes. Maybe he's insecure or something, I think that he's just shy. She saw that there was a television in the corner, there was a newscaster talking about the news of the day.

The next newscaster that came on was standing in front of the Gallo Luxury lodge, where there was yellow caution tape wrapped around the outside of the building. The newscaster, said there were three people murdered just hours ago here. The murderer still hasn't been found, if you see this man call our tip line.

A k-9 unit has been brought into the area to look for him, the Police Chief is hoping that he's found today. The lodge is going to reopen again after two days. The owner of the lodge just left moments ago, he was saddened to hear what happened. Now onto sports, then she looked away from the television.

She saw a young woman walk in with a baby in her arms, she had an unpleasant look on her face. She just happened look out the window and seen a Fire Engine go by. I'm sorry for taking so long to deliver your coffee to you, but the coffee maker wasn't working. It's alright you don't have to explain yourself.

What was so interesting on the television?

A murder story.

Look there's a basketball game on now, I haven't watched a basketball game in so long. You don't look interested in anything that I'm saying, you're just stirring your coffee with the spoon and not saying anything.

You really should think about reading your menu instead of looking off into space. The waiter's going to be back soon and ask what you want to eat. I'm not very hungry though, you have to at least order something.

Is it something I said?

No.

There are so many dinner entrees, and side dishes on this menu. Written in small words under this entree it says fat free, don't order that that's for someone on a diet. I haven't had stewed tomatoes in a while. If I were you I'd look under the sandwiches section of the menu. The Mac and cheese here is always good.

You'll have to make a decision soon, stop rushing me. She began to play with her hair, and was no longer looking at him. You can get your hand away from me. I know what I'm going to order, and so do my buddies. The waiter was holding the coffee pot, and looking over at the television.

A man feverishly walked by and bumped into the waiters shoulder, causing him to drop the coffee pot. Coffee went all over the floor, and everyone was staring at him. You people can stop looking at me now, it wasn't all my fault.

Some elderly woman spoke up and said, you don't have to speak with an attitude like that. The waiter never said anything back to her, he just continued on what he was doing.

He took the mop out of the closet, and took it over to where the mess was and began mopping it up. One of the other waiters came over to him and whispered something in his ear.

She heard the other guys ordering their food, and took another quick look at the menu. The waiter turned and looked at her, I would like a burrito and French fries. That burrito comes with salsa, you can order one more thing with that. He pointed to the sides on the menu, I'll have the stewed tomatoes.

I'll be back with your order shortly. Coming from somewhere nearby, someone was cracking their gum in their mouth. A Police Officer walked in, he was whistling and observing everyone. After several minutes of standing there, the Officer was becoming impatient. Hello I've been waiting here patiently.

Don't worry Sir, you'll be seated soon the waiters are all busy at the moment. He crossed his arms and began whistling again. Eventually a waiter got to him, and took him over to a table. You're being awfully cold to me, and it's getting old.

"Aren't you going to thank me for this?"

"Yes," I will.

You drank your coffee awfully fast, you seem a bit nervous. I won't be leaving here with you, or those other guys. Eventually the waiter came over with their food, Ma'am your stewed tomatoes will be out soon.

"Would you like some ketchup?"

"Yes," I would please.

The waiter came back with a small bottle of ketchup, and handed it to her. She put some ketchup on her plate, and picked up a French fry and eat it. While her friend was munching on a hamburger. You have a pile of fries on that plate, I hope that you're hungry.

"Don't you fellas like vegetables?

"No."

"Where's your stewed tomatoes?"

"They weren't brought out yet."

"How's your burger?"

"It tastes great thanks."

My French fries are awfully salted, it just makes the coffee go down better. I think we should have a fudge Sunday for desert.

She stopped eating and got up and walked over to the bathroom. She entered the bathroom and closed the door behind her and turned on the light and looked into the mirror. She straightened out her shirt, and began playing with their hair. She grabbed a paper towel, and wiped the sweat off of her forehead. She turned on the water, and began washing her hands.

She finished up in the bathroom, and walked back to the table. Her eyes were glued to the television again, the newscaster was standing at the lodge again. When she heard that the murderer at large was caught, she felt herself relax. They soon finished eating, and the waiter brought the check.

One of them paid the bill, and they walked out of the place. I can't say that it was very enjoyable with you, that's because I don't like you. You should come home with me, I have a nice comfy couch and a big screen television. That's not going to make me anymore interested, you and the other guys should get going now.

Just leave me here, and I'll be fine. If you ask me one more time I'm going to tell the Policeman. They got on their bicycles and rode away. She sat down on the bench in front of the diner, and watched many people come and go. Several birds flew overhead, and there was a squirrel crawling up the nearby tree. A car pulled out of the parking lot burning up its tires, and crashed into a parked car along the street. Three joggers ran by, and were smiling, they had their headphones on.

A man came walking down the street with his two dogs. He stopped and took out his phone and began staring into it. A woman pushing a stroller was coming towards him, excuse me Sir I'm coming through. You're not even paying attention to me, the man finally stopped looking at his phone and let her pass.

One of the man's dogs was pulling on his leash, and began barking at the other people who walked by. One of the women looked up at him, your dog is awfully noisy. You should have kept him at home.

"How long have you had him for?"

"For three years now."

You should spend more time with your dog.

"Are you a dog trainer or something?"

"No," I'm not.

Those two talked for several more minutes, then went their separate ways. A taxi pulled up to the curve, and someone got out of it and walked over to the diner. He was wearing a fine suit, and had a smile on his face.

"Are you okay there Ma'am?"

"Yes," I am.

She quickly ran over to the taxi before it left.

"Can you take me to the sandwich shop?"

"Yes," I will.

She quickly got in, and they drove off. Soon they arrived at the sandwich shop, it will be fourteen dollars then. She carefully handed him the money and got out of the car it and walked over to the shop. She entered the shop, and took a seat. There was one man standing behind the counter, taking peoples orders. She was content just watching the people.

The door opened and she was surprised to see who it was, it was her husband. I'm so glad to see you again, I thought I'd never see you again. I tried calling you but nothing happened, that's because my phone ran out of battery. I thought that the murder got ahold of you. I went back to sleep after you left, I kind of figured that. You're shaking honey, it's because I'm so excited to see you.

"Where were you before you came here?"

"At the diner."

“So you already ate?”

“Yes,” I did.

I've been thinking about a tuna fish sandwich all day. If you're that hungry then you should get a large.

“Are you going to get chips with it?”

“Yes”

As I was driving here, someone pulled out in front of me. I saw some protesters standing beside the street, waving their signs. I took all back roads to get here, there was less traffic that way. I saw a dad carrying his son in his arms, and the little boy had the biggest smile on his face.

“Would you like an ice cream cone?”

“No,” thanks.

You know how good the ice cream is here.

“Would you share a bottle of wine with me?”

“I gladly will.”

Don't worry it's the kind that you like, I wasn't worried Dear. I can't believe how fast, he brought out my meal. You just enjoy that Dear, I'll be right here looking out the window. I can tell that you're going to need some napkins, let me get some for you. She walked up to the front counter, and grabbed a handful of napkins and brought it back to the table. It's nice to see you enjoying your meal, I'm thoroughly enjoying it.

Being around you makes even better, thanks Dear. Would you like to open the wine or shall I? I will. You have done a lot for me over the past week, so now I'm going to help you. This brings to memory, that time when I opened up a bottle of campaign and the cork flew up and hit me in the nose. You laughed so hard you almost fell over, and my Uncle didn't say a thing.

They continued their dinner conversation, and he finished up his meal and the wine. They soon left and went to a local hotel for the night. Once there they continued their conversation, and got comfortable in bed and fell asleep. Back at cliffhanger lodge, the conversation continued.

I appreciate you looking for me and I hope that Callie and the kid are still out there and are just lost. I'm sorry to say this Alvin but if they are still outside overnight, they would probably freeze to death, and we will never find them alive again. Don't think so negatively, maybe Callie knows how to build and start a fire.

No, I don't think she would know how. If she comes back tomorrow let me know Alvin. I will let you know. Now I have to get going, it's six thirty already and my shift is over at nine o clock. It's been nice to meet you, likewise.

"Do you live here at the lodge?"

"Yes," I do live here.

"Did you show me your room?"

"Yes," I showed it to you briefly.

"Do you have anything in your room that I should be concerned about?"

"No," Officer

I have my carry permit with me wherever I go, and I don't let loaded firearms sitting around. I'm going to get going, bye now. Alvin remained sitting in his comfy office chair.

All of a sudden, his phone rang, he quickly picked it up and Leo answered.

"How's your night going?"

"It's going good thanks for asking"

"How are you?"

"I'm doing good too."

I have good news for you.

"What it is?"

"I will be arriving at your lodge tomorrow at eleven o clock."

That's just wonderful, I happy to hear that. I will now go back to the spare bedroom and get it ready for you.

"Is there a lot of work to be done to the spare room?"

"No," Leo, it won't take me long to get all the papers and magazines off of the mattress.

I'm going to take the vacuum cleaner, right now and clean the rooms carpet while I'm thinking about it. I will let you go, and I will see you tomorrow. Alvin walked into the spare bedroom and didn't see the vacuum where he had placed it before, the room was dark.

He flicked the light switch and the one bright light lit up. He opened up the closet and looked inside of it, there were boxes and other papers laying all around in the closet. There was a trash can that was full of shredded paperwork from years before.

He quickly took the trash can out of the closet and placed in the doorway. He went further into the closet and came across the vacuum cleaner, the vacuum clean cord was all wrapped up and there was something sticky on the cord. Alvin couldn't figure out where or why the cord had something sticky on it.

He was able to get the vacuum cleaner out of the closet and was sweating. He wiped his forehead and let out a sigh. He thought to himself that was a lot of work getting out the vacuum cleaner. He then thought to himself I hope that the vacuum cleaner still works.

Alvin would buy the best vacuums and cleaning supplies. He took the attachments off of the vacuum and placed them on the floor beside them the vacuum. He looked for a place to plug in the vacuum and found a place. He quickly plugged it in and then went on to look for the on and off switch on the vacuum.

He pressed in the on and off switch and it came on. The noise that it made was loud and he wasn't used to the noise. He walked over to the bed and saw that there was a dead ant on the mattress.

Chapter Five: The Search

He didn't like knowing that there was a dead ant on the mattress. He was feeling so tired and he leaned over and fell onto the bed and began to feel like he was going to fall asleep. He opened his eyes for a brief moment then fell asleep.

He happened to wake up and looked over at the clock on the wall and it showed that it was four thirty in the morning. He quickly got up and saw that he was wearing the same clothes that he was wearing from yesterday. He walked over by the vacuum and saw that it was still plugged in and he turned it on and began to sweep the carpet. It didn't take him long to sweep the whole floor.

After he was done he took a five-minute break and sat on the bed. He was so hungry for a bagel and that's all that he could think about. He bent down and unplugged the vacuum cleaner and walked down the hallway to the kitchen. The kitchen was so dark that he could barely see, so he switched on the light and took a look around.

He saw that there was one bagel left, and he opened the one drawer next to the cabinet and brought out a butter knife. He cut the bagel in half and began to butter it up. It didn't take him long to consume the bagel. He walked over to the thermostat, and it read that it was seventy-two degrees. He opened up the blind and looked outside, even though it was still dark outside.

Alvin thought to himself I hope that Callie and the kid come back this morning. He saw that the sun was beginning to rise up over the mountains. He looked down at his watch and it showed that it was five in the morning, and Alvin thought that the time was moving by so slowly.

He was feeling bored, so he sat down on the couch in the main room by the front of the lodge. He didn't want to sit in his office chair and remained sitting on the couch. He looked down at the magazines on the coffee table, and there were four magazines laying there. Each magazine had a different topic, he reached down and picked up a hunting magazine. It had a white tail buck on the cover of it.

The buck was a five pointer, and this made him interested in reading the magazine. He carefully pages through the magazine. Each page was filled with pictures and the different hunting products that he could purchase. Although Alvin doesn't like to purchase anything from hunting magazines, he would rather just go to the hunting store and look around himself.

A short article about food plots caught his attention, and he read two paragraphs then went paging on through the magazine. This particular magazine was much thicker than the other magazines.

He came across a four-wheeler ad, it said come in today and check out our new rides. Our rides are good and dependable and made for fun. He liked looking at the pictures of the new four wheelers, but soon got bored of it and turned the page.

He thought to himself all I'm doing is wasting time while Callie and the poor kid is freezing out there. He heard something hit the side of the lodge by the window. He looked out and it was just beginning to get light outside. He looked closer and saw that there was an old shovel that was thrown against the wall by the window. He thought to himself well this is strange I wonder what's going on.

Alvin grabbed his coat from the coat hanger by the door and walked outside. He could immediately feel the cold winter air, and this caused his face to turn red. He walked over by the shovel and picked it up and on the bottom of the shovel was dried blood and it was bent. He wasn't sure what to do next so, he looked behind and walked halfway around the lodge outside.

There was no sign of anyone around, he scratched his head and thought that perhaps he was going crazy. He walked up towards the large shed. He remembered locking up the shed that night and saw it was opened.

He was feeling suspicious and thought to himself I better go back in and get my gun. But he was too lazy to run back inside the lodge. He continued on walking towards the opened shed.

Once he was right in front of the shed, he pulled out his flashlight and was ready to shine it in the shed. Once he threw open both doors, he was expecting for someone or something to come out after him, but nothing happened. All he saw were the snow cat and the four snow machines.

He thought that he had heard something, so he walked towards the back of the snow cat and to his horror, there was a man sitting in the snow cat fast asleep. Alvin had never seen this man before, Alvin slowly approached the snow cat, the man was still fast asleep. He was leaning over on the driver's side door.

Alvin knew that he couldn't just open the driver's side door, or the man may wake up. He could hear the man snoring, the man didn't appear to have a gun or anything like that. He just didn't understand where the shovel had come from. The blood on the shovel hadn't been there before.

This made the mystery increasingly concerning to Alvin. Alvin forgot to turn off the flashlight and the guy must of saw the flash of the flashlights light and he pulled his head up and stared down Alvin. He stared at Alvin for a good two minutes then tried to quickly get out of the snow cat. Not so fast buddy,

      "Alvin took the man down and held him face down on the hard floor."

      "Now tell me what is your name?"

      "My name is Frank"

      "Why do you care what my name is?"

      "You are trespassing on my land, and I don't appreciate it Mister."

      "Who are you?"

      "My name is Alvin"

I'm the owner of this lodge.

"Where did you come from?"

I walked here from the other side of the mountain.

"Why?"

I just wanted to explore the area. I don't believe you, now tell me the reason or I will twist your wrists or ankles.

"I killed two people, oh really."

"Who were they?"

The one was a women and the other was a little who looked like he was maybe just ten years old.

"How dare you?"

"What did they do to you?"

They had built a fire and the women, saw me walking along and told me to get away from her. I kept on walking closer, and she grabbed my arms and threw a stick at me, I dodged it and took her down in a choke lock around the throat.

"What did the kid do?"

"He jumped on my back and began punching me."

I hit him in the face twice and he fell onto his back. There was an old shovel laying on the ground next to where the women was, and that's what I used to kill her. I had left go of her and she tried to run away from me, and I hit her in the head once with the shovel knocking her down into the deep snow.

"Where did the little boy go?"

"He didn't recover from me hitting him in the face."

The women fell down face down into the snow and was bleeding from the top of her head. She could barely even move so I hit her again and she then laid there motionless and blood continued to run down her face and her eyes closed and she stopped breathing and I then ran over to where the little boy was laying and struck him in the head with shovel and then he was motionless.

"What did you do with the bodies?"

"Why do you care?"

I dug one small hole and threw there both bodies in it and threw some snow over their bodies.

"You are sick man, what's your problem?"

"I don't have a problem I'm a killer and will always murder people."

No, you won't, you are going to be under arrest for murder. I'm going to call the authorities on you, now stay on the ground until I can get my phone out.

"You think that I'm going to let you get your phone?"

"You're wrong, I'm going to put up a fight and you won't win."

We shall see about that, you're hurting my back, by holding me down like that, just be quiet, I don't care what you have to say anymore.

"Why don't you take me into the lodge where it is warm?"

"No," you're a murder and murders aren't allowed in my lodge.

"How are you going to remain out here in the cold?"

"I don't care about the cold."

You sure seem to care about the cold, you aren't acting like a man at all.

"What are you anyway?"

"You seem wimpy to me, is that so."

You're just a rich man that don't care about the middle class. I'm a kind man, but I don't think it's right what you did. I'm surprised that you weren't arrested sooner.

"Have you killed anyone else before?"

"No," but I killed someone's dog.

"What don't you like dogs?"

"No," I don't

I don't care about having a dog either. Your clothes are all torn, and you stink, and it looks like you haven't shaved in years. Now you are going to make fun of how I look. You are just a loser, No, I'm not. Now you are making me angry, please get off of me.

"How did you get into the shed?"

I used the shovel to smash the lock and the doors came open easily and I walked in.

"How did you get into my snow cat?"

"The keys were still in the ignition."

"What?"

"Elmer should not have left the keys in the ignition."

I'm going to have to have a talk with him when I see him.

Who's Elmer?

He's, my repairman.

Who was the women that I killed, that women had a name; her name was Callie, and the little boys name was Harmon. They were both too young to die.

"Why did you throw the shovel at the side of the lodge?"

"To get your attention"

I'm glad that the wall of my lodge wasn't damaged. You know, all you are doing is just talking, you're not taking any action to fight me. I don't want to keep on fighting with you.

"Do you have any plans for the day today?"

"I'm not going to answer that, and now I'm calling the Police."

Go ahead, don't let me stop you. You're an ugly man. Your hair's down to your shoulders, and you have bad body odor. Alvin was quickly able to get his phone out and dialed Robs number. He kept his body on top of Frank's body and didn't let up.

The phone kept on ringing and nobody picked up, eventually the answering machine picked up. It said please leave a message and beeped. Alvin said I need help as soon as possible and then hung up.

"What happened?"

"Didn't anyone pick up?"

Chapter Six: Coming To A Close

"Be quite."

My stomach's beginning to hurt, while I lay on the ground. Now please let me up.

"How can I trust you?"

"I don't know."

"Do you have any hand cuffs on you?"

"No," I don't I just have, a zip tie that I found that was in my back pocket.

Hold your wrists together and let me tie them together. Now you are listening to me, you and I are going to stay out in the cold until the Police get here. Alvin looked down at his watch and saw that it was going on ten thirty and soon Leo is going to show up.

"Who's Leo?"

"You know you are asking me too many questions."

He's just my Butler, enough with the questions

"What happened to your mom and dad?"

"I murdered them both and I won't tell you about how I killed them."

You remind me of a child, to let you know I'm no child and leave me alone. You're a real bad man and killing someone at all is wrong. Alvin's phone began to ring, and Alvin answered it, Rob was on the other line. I just got your message. I'm going to come out now, keep him in restraint until I get there.

Within fifteen minutes Rob pulled into the driveway, Alvin hung up his phone and waited until Rob came over. Frank's eyes got all big and his jaw dropped, I didn't want to go to jail, just be quiet Mister, hi, Rob.

"Who's this here"

"Frank and he's a murder"

"How do you know?"

He told me, and I have the murder weapon right here. It's this bloody shovel leaning up against the lodge. Alvin heard a truck pull up. I wasn't sure who it was at first. So this man Frank murdered Callie and the kid.

Sir, you are coming with me, you are under arrest and don't fight me or I will knock you out. Those are fighting words, and with that comment Rob kicked up some snow in Frank's face.

> "Why did you have to do that?"

> "For your behavior"

I'm going to put you away for the rest of your life. I can't stand you; I can't believe that they let you be a Police Officer. Stop talking I'm not in a good mood. I'm going to take Frank and the murder weapon down to the station.

I will talk to you later, bye good luck. Rob took Frank around the side of the lodge back to the parking lot. Alvin quickly locked up the shed and continued to walk back to the lodge. He opened the door and walked in and saw that someone was standing by the front desk.

> "Who are you?"

> "I'm Leo, it's great to have finally met you"

> "Who was the Policeman walking along with, that's another story?"

> "I'm glad to see that you got here safe and sound."

> "How did you find the lodge?"

> "I just used my GPS to get here."

> "Where's my room?"

> "It's the third room off to the right."

> "Thank you"

> "Aren't you going to talk to me before you go back to your room?"

> "I would like to, but I have a lot of things I have to carry back to my room."

I will be back don't worry.

> "Would you like me to help you carry some of those suitcases?"

> "No," thank you.

Just sit back down at your desk and I will be back soon. Alvin felt so uptight, so he walked into the middle living room and opened the cabinet and took out the bottle of brandy and didn't even bother to take out a shot glass.

He just picked up the whole bottle and took a drink. When he was done taking a sip, he put it away and returned to his desk. Yes, I thought that you said the whole spare room was cleaned out and ready.

"How comes there are some boxes still in here?"

"I don't know, just give me a minute and I will come and take all the boxes out of there."

Leo came walking out of the room and walked back towards Alvin's desk.

"Are you okay?"

"Yes," I love this lodge

It's a bit larger than I thought it was, I'm going to love sleeping here, it will be nice and quiet and not loud like the city is at night. I lived by a busy road, and cars and tractor trailers would always be driving past.

"Do you see a lot of wildlife around here?"

"Very rarely."

This is because there are a lot of people that come here to ski, and they make a lot of noise.

"Have you seen any bears around here?"

"No."

I know that there are some mountain lions that live around here.

Do you like to go for long walks around your property?"

"No," I don't.

It gets so cold outside around here in the winter months.

I like the cold so it's perfect for me.

"How was your plane ride here?"

"It wasn't so good."

"Why's that?"

"We had experienced a lot of turbulence."

I got a big bruise on my right shoulder, from being thrown against the passenger side door. That must have hurt, let me show you, and Leo pulled back his long sleeve shirt. Here's the black and blue mark on my shoulder, that looks painful.

"Does it still hurt?"

"No," it just really aches.

"Do you have any pain rub for my shoulder?"

"I probably have some pain creme left."

"I will have to check in the back medicine cabinet."

I'll be right back, just give me a moment okay. Alvin walked to towards the back of the lodge. He was halfway down the hallway, and he happened to look in the control room and saw that one of the eight monitors wasn't on. However, he just ignored it and went to the cabinet in the back of the lodge.

He bent down on one knee and opened the lower cabinet. A few packs of band aids, fell out onto the floor. Alvin quickly picked them up and placed them back in the cabinet. He looked in the next cabinet and found a container of pain creme, he thought this creme will be just perfect for Leo. He happened to look behind him and Leo was standing there.

I just wanted to see what you were doing. You almost scared me standing behind me. I'm sorry, I didn't mean to scare you. It's okay, but don't do it again, you know that I use pain creme at home. Alvin handed Leo the container of creme, and he gently applied it to his sore shoulder, that feels much better.

"What do you like to do?"

"I like to shoot guns and spend some time riding on the snow machine."

"How about you?"

"I like to spend time with my close friends and go out to eat."

"Is there a MacDougall's around here?"

"Yes," there is, it's about twenty-two minutes away from here.

I like to get egg and bacon sandwiches every other day.

“Do you like MacDougall's food?”

“No,” I can't say that I do.

“Are you a health food junky?”

“No,” I'm not

I just prefer to eat healthy, and it makes me feel better.

“Did you ever see the movie Big-size me?”

“No,” I can't say that I have.

Let me tell you about it, hey look it's snowing outside. The movie's about a man who eats nothing but junk food from MacDougall. So what? So after he just eats McDougall food for a week, he became deathly ill.

I don't overdo it. I know my body and would never endanger myself. I can tell that you and I are going to get along just fine. Later that afternoon Leo and Alvin had a few drinks together and wrapped up the day.